My Mindful Walk
with Grandma

Sheri Mabry

illustrated by Wazza Pink

Albert Whitman & Company ∿ Chicago, Illinois

To my brothers, Bill and John, for being on the path with me; the living planet,
for the beauty along the path; and for my practice, for guiding me home—SM

For you, my dear Grandma. Hope you can find peace wherever you are now.
Thank you for all the good things you brought me in my life. And for all the busy people
around the world, please enjoy every moment before it passes.—WP

Library of Congress Cataloging-in-Publication data is on file with the publisher.

Text copyright © 2020 by Sheri Mabry
Illustrations copyright © 2020 by Albert Whitman & Company
Illustrations by Wazza Pink
First published in the United States of America in 2020 by Albert Whitman & Company
ISBN 978-0-8075-7072-2 (hardcover)
ISBN 978-0-8075-7073-9 (ebook)
Printed in China
10 9 8 7 6 5 4 3 2 1 WKT 24 23 22 21 20 19

Design by Aphelandra Messer

For more information about Albert Whitman & Company,
visit our website at www.albertwhitman.com.

I wake up before the sun. I hold my
breath and listen, hoping to hear the
loons. But I only hear the sparrows
outside my window.

Each spring, when the trilliums peek up, Grandma and I hike through the woods to see if the loons have returned yet. Grandma does her whistle. Sometimes the loons answer back.

I reach for my stone and slide it into my pocket, then I burst out the screen door. I can't wait to get to the lake!

"Looks like the sun squirted paint right into the corners of the sky," Grandma says softly. "Wonder what other surprises we will find."

Grandma doesn't know it, but I have a surprise of my own!

Sssppp. Slisshhhhh.

"Listen to the new leaves," says Grandma.

She slows down and looks up. But I don't.

I am too excited to get to my surprise.

We keep hiking. I skip ahead.

Splash! My socks get wet. *Splash!* *Splash!* My socks get wetter. When I'm with Grandma, I can even stomp in the mud, and she doesn't tell me not to.

"Do you hear it?" asks Grandma.
My feet stop moving so fast.
But I don't hear anything except
the excited surprise
jumping around in
my head.

I crawl over logs and peek under rocks.

Grandma stays on the trail.

I come back and hold her hand.

"Are we almost there?" I ask.

"Ah, but if we keep looking for *there*, we will miss what is *right here*."

Grandma stops. She squeezes my hand.

So I stop too. I reach in my pocket and hold my stone. I close my eyes. I can feel it better now. The stone is heavy and smooth and cool between my fingers. With my eyes closed and my feet still, my ears start to work better too.

I say quietly, "I hear the leaves now, Grandma. It's like they are dancing around on the trees."

"It does sound like a leaf dance," Grandma whispers back. "There are lots of forest surprises to be a part of." She takes a breath. So I do too.

My belly fills with a big breath. When I let it go, my breath floats out and dances with the breeze in the leaves.

In and out, I breathe.

In and out, the leaves dance.

And soon my fluttery thoughts about racing to the lake blow away.

I hear katydids and spring peepers and
crickets chirping and humming and buzzing.
I smell pine cones and ferns.
Sun heats my cheeks.
My toes are wet and cold in my socks.
Grandma's hand is warm and soft.

I slowly open my eyes.

And there, like tiny surprises I didn't see
before, are spring flowers covering the path!
     Where before I only saw
trees and bushes, bits of blue
now peek through the branches.
We are at the lake!

This is the place. It's where Grandma whistles.
And where the loons call back. Sometimes.

Now it's my turn.

"I have a surprise for you, Grandma!" I curl my
hands together. I fill my chest with air. I blow hard.
But it only goes, *whoosh*. My heart is fluttering
hummingbird fast. I blow harder…

but still nothing.

Grandma squeezes my shoulder. So I stop.
I close my eyes, reach in my pocket, and
hold the cool smoothness again.
I take a deep belly breath, in and out.
Slowly. In and out.

I listen and smell and hear everything just as it is, *right now*.
I try the whistle once more.

This time
softer,
slower.

And it comes!

It sounds like Grandma's whistle. And it sounds like
the loon's call. But it's all mine, floating in the leaves.
Grandma's smile is big. Her hug is bigger.

She sits against the giant pine. I settle next to her like I do when she reads to me on the porch during a summer rain. I smell her flannel shirt as she pulls me close. My head rests on her shoulder.

Then, off in the distance, it begins. Starting out soft, the sound grows and grows until it wraps all around us…

OHHOOOEEOOO

"The loons! They are back! Grandma. She…*answered me!*"

Grandma squeezes me into a hug.
"It's about time to be getting
back to the cabin. You can share
your surprise with Grandpa!"
A flutter of *excitement* bubbles up
as I think about telling Grandpa.
But I don't want to go just yet.

With the stone in my pocket,
the loon's call in the air,
snug in Grandma's hug,

I am…

right here, right now.

Author's Note

Did you notice that the young girl in the story was so excited about her surprise, that she was missing what was happening all around her? Learning to be present in the moment is what mindfulness is about, and can help you enjoy each moment more. It can also help you feel calmer and more peaceful.

The first step to being mindful is to belly breathe. Fill your belly up like a balloon when you breathe in (inhale), and allow your belly to empty of the breath as you breathe out (exhale). This will help you feel calmer right away. Next, close your eyes and begin to think about your breath. Imagine the air coming in through your nose, then down through your lungs and filling up your belly, and then imagine it coming back out. Keep thinking about your breath like this. Your thoughts might like to wander, but gently tell your thoughts to come back to the breath. You can use this to help you anytime you are feeling anxious or worried.

Next, start noticing what is happening in the present moment, right here and now! Listen to the sounds, one by one. Take in the smells, one by one. Feel what your body is feeling.

Now, allow yourself to feel grateful as you bring your thoughts back to your breath. Being grateful means to feel thankful about the moment. This can help you feel calmer and happier too.

Nature is a wonderful place to practice mindfulness, because breathing fresh air, connecting to earth, and being around trees and wildlife can help us be healthy, calm, and peaceful. And remember, if you are calm and peaceful in the forest…you will notice things you wouldn't if you were moving quickly and making lots of noise. It is not only better for you, but it is better for the wilderness if you look and listen peacefully, and leave things just how they are. Right here, right now.

The Loon Whistle

If you'd like to learn how to do the loon whistle, follow the instructions below. Like the girl in the story, it might take a bit of practice before you get a true whistle to come out. Don't give up. Keep trying and trying. Once you are able to do the whistle, it will be a moment that you can share with someone special.

How to do the loon whistle:

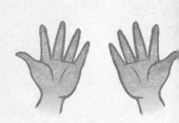

1. Begin by putting both hands out in front of you. Your palms are facing you.

2. Next, squeeze the sides of your right four fingers together (not your thumb) and place these fingers onto the skin between your left thumb and pointer finger. Look at the illustration, and notice how the hands are cupped.

3. With your hands cupped, slide them closed.

4. Press your two thumbs together, which are facing you, and lay them on top of the right pointer finger.

5. Now, leave a little space between your thumbs. Your thumbs are bent a little.

6. Place your lower lip at the bottom of the bend, and your upper lip at the top of the bend.

7. Blow slowly. If you blow hard, it won't work. If you blow slowly, it will. This takes a lot of practice, so don't give up. Wiggle your hands and fingers around a bit; adjust your lips a little. Soon you will find the perfect position. Have patience, and before you know it, you'll be doing the whistle of the woods!